JOSEFINA LEARNS A LESSON

A SCHOOL STORY

BY VALERIE TRIPP

ILLUSTRATIONS JEAN-PAUL TIBBLES

VIGNETTES SUSAN McALILEY

PLEASANT COMPANY

Printed in the United States of America.
98 99 00 01 02 WCT 10 9 8 7 6 5 4

The American Girls Collection®, Josefina™, and Josefina Montoya™
are trademarks of Pleasant Company.

PERMISSIONS & PICTURE CREDITS
Grateful acknowledgment is made to the following for permission to quote previously
published material: p. 42—Enrique R. Lamadrid (excerpt from "Las mañanitas / Little morning
song" in *Tesoros del espíritu: A portrait in sound of Hispanic New Mexico,* University of
New Mexico Press, © 1994 Enrique R. Lamadrid); p. 56—University of Oklahoma Press
(verse published in *The Folklore of Spain in the American Southwest,* by Aurelio M. Espinosa,
edited by J. Manuel Espinosa, © 1985 University of Oklahoma Press, Norman,
Publishing Division of the University).

The following individuals and organizations have generously given permission to reprint
illustrations contained in "Looking Back": pp. 62-63—Brooklyn Museum of Art 41.1275.167
(writing desk); Benemérita Universidad Autónoma de Puebla (silabario); Museum of
New Mexico (inkwell); pp. 64-65—documents from Spanish Archives of New Mexico,
Series II, #137b, #160, #1249, New Mexico State Records Center & Archives (signatures);
Museum of New Mexico, neg. #147058 (girl sewing); courtesy George Ancona, Santa Fe, NM
(man and boy working); pp. 66-67—courtesy, The Bancroft Library, University of
California, Berkeley (musician).

Edited by Peg Ross
Designed by Mark Macauley, Myland McRevey, Laura Moberly, and Jane S. Varda
Art Directed by Jane S. Varda

Library of Congress Cataloging-in-Publication Data

Tripp, Valerie, 1951-
Josefina learns a lesson : a school story / by Valerie Tripp ;
illustrations, Jean-Paul Tibbles ; vignettes, Susan McAliley. — 1st ed.
p. cm. — (The American girls collection)
Summary: Josefina and her sisters distrust learning to read and write,
as well as other changes their Tía Dolores is bringing to the household,
because they fear they will lose their memories of their mother.
ISBN 1-56247-518-5. — ISBN 1-56247-517-7 (pbk.)
[1. Ranch life—New Mexico—Fiction. 2. Mexican Americans—Fiction.
3. Sisters—Fiction. 4. Aunts—Fiction. 5. New Mexico—History—To 1848—Fiction.]
I. Tibbles, Jean-Paul, ill. II. McAliley, Susan. III. Title. IV. Series.
PZ7.T7363Jo 1997 [Fic]—dc21 97-3450 CIP AC

TO MY MOTHER,
KATHLEEN MARTIN TRIPP
WITH LOVE

Josefina and her family speak Spanish, so you'll see some Spanish words in this book. If you can't tell what a word means from reading the story or looking at the illustrations, you can turn to the "Glossary of Spanish Words" that begins on page 68. It will tell you what the word means and how to pronounce it.

Remember that in Spanish, "j" is pronounced like "h." That means Josefina's name is pronounced "ho-seh-FEE-nah."

TABLE OF CONTENTS

PAPÁ
*Josefina's father, who
guides his family
and his rancho with
quiet strength.*

ANA
*Josefina's oldest sister,
who is married and has
two little boys.*

JOSEFINA
*A nine-year-old girl
whose heart and hopes
are as big as the
New Mexico sky.*

FRANCISCA
*Josefina's fifteen-year-old
sister, who is headstrong
and impatient.*

CLARA
*Josefina's practical,
sensible sister, who is
twelve years old.*

TÍA DOLORES
*Josefina's aunt, who
has lived far away in
Mexico City for ten years.*

TERESITA
*Tía Dolores's servant,
an excellent weaver.*

CHAPTER ONE

LIGHT AND SHADOW

"María Josefina Montoya!" said Tía Dolores happily. "How beautiful you look!"

Josefina blushed and smiled at her aunt. "*Gracias*," she said. She smoothed the long skirt of her new dress with both hands. The cotton material felt soft and light. Josefina rose up on her toes and spun, just for the sheer pleasure of it. She was very proud of her dress, which she had just finished hemming. She had never had a dress made in this elegant, new, high-waisted style before. Tía Dolores had given Josefina and each of her sisters some material. Josefina's material was a pretty yellow, with narrow stripes and tiny berries on it. She had

1

cut her material carefully, the way Mamá had taught her. Then stitch by tiny stitch, she had sewn her dress together all by herself. Now, as she spun around, the hearth fire cast a pattern of light and shadow swooping across the dress like a flock of fluttering birds.

Josefina stopped spinning and sighed with peaceful contentment. It was a rainy evening in October. Josefina and her three older sisters, Ana, Francisca, and Clara, were sewing in front of the fire in the family *sala*. Tía Dolores was helping them. They were all glad of the fire's warmth as well as its cheerful brightness. A steady, heavy rain was falling outside, but inside it was cozy. The thick, whitewashed *adobe* walls kept out the cold and took on a rosy glow from the firelight.

Tía Dolores sat next to Clara. "Don't use such a long thread in your needle," she advised Clara gently. "It might tangle."

Josefina grinned. "Remember, Clara?" she said. "Mamá used to say, 'If you make your thread too long, the devil will catch on to the end of it!'"

All the sisters smiled and nodded, and Tía

Dolores said, "I remember your mamá saying that to me when we were young girls learning to sew!"

Tía Dolores was smiling. But Josefina saw that her eyes were sad, and she knew that Tía Dolores was missing Mamá.

Tía Dolores was Mamá's sister. Mamá had died more than a year ago. Josefina and her sisters thought of Mamá every day, with longing and love. Every day, the girls tried to do their chores the way Mamá had taught them to. They tried to be as respectful, hardworking, and obedient as she would have wished them to be. Every day, they recalled her wise and funny sayings and songs. And every day, they remembered her in their prayers.

The first year after Mamá's death, the four girls had struggled hard to run the household. Then, at the end of the summer, Tía Dolores had come to visit. She was on her way home to Santa Fe from Mexico City, where she had been living for ten years. During her visit, the girls had realized how much they needed someone like her—someone to help them and teach them as Mamá used to do. Tía Dolores

kindly agreed to come live on the *rancho* for a while. She went to Santa Fe to see her parents for a month. But she kept her promise and returned to the rancho with her servant Teresita in time to help with the harvest. Tía Dolores had been back for two weeks now, and Josefina was glad.

As Clara shortened her thread, she looked at Josefina's dress. "You'll get a lot of good wear out of that dress," she said. Clara was next to Josefina in age. She was sensible and straightforward. "It was a good idea to make it too long. That way you can grow into it."

"Oh, dear!" said Josefina, looking at her hem. "Is my dress too long?"

"Not at all. It's perfect," said Ana in her tenderhearted way. She was the oldest sister, already grown up and married. "You've done a fine job, Josefina. And you are the first one of us to finish." Ana had not even begun her dress yet. She had decided to make vests for her two little boys first.

Francisca, the second oldest sister, sighed a huge sigh. "I'm far from finishing my dress," she said. "I've still so much to do."

"You shouldn't have chosen such a fancy

dress pattern," said Clara, pricking her material with the sharp needle. Tía Dolores had given Francisca a sewing diary that showed all the latest styles from Mexico City, and the girls had each chosen a dress pattern to follow. Clara was making a dress that was plain and simple. She prided herself on being practical and often felt called upon to point it out when someone else wasn't. That someone was usually Francisca.

Francisca had chosen an elaborate pattern from the sewing diary. She'd begun enthusiastically. She cut into the material boldly, talking all the while about how splendid her dress would be. But the long, slow work of sewing the pieces together bored Francisca. She complained every stitch of the way. "I'll never finish my dress," she said now, "unless someone helps me with this endless stitching." She glanced sideways at Tía Dolores.

Josefina saw the sideways look. She knew that Francisca wanted Tía Dolores to sew for her. But Tía Dolores calmly continued her own sewing. She said nothing, even when Francisca sighed loudly again. Josefina was not surprised. In the last two weeks, she had learned that Tía Dolores was always willing to give help and advice. But she would not do the girls' work for them.

A few days ago, Josefina and Tía Dolores had worked together in the corner of the back courtyard where Mamá's flowers grew. Tía Dolores showed Josefina how to prepare the flowers for the winter. She explained how to cut back the dead stems and cover the earth with leaves to protect it from ice and snow. She watched with care to be sure Josefina was doing everything correctly. Tía Dolores helped, but she made it clear that the flowers were Josefina's responsibility. "I want you to know how to care for them by yourself after I leave," she'd said. "I know you can do it. I have faith in you."

Tía Dolores worked hard teaching, and she expected the girls to work hard learning. "Our energies and abilities are gifts from God," she often said. "He means for us to put them to good use." Sometimes Josefina thought that perhaps Tía Dolores had a little too *much* faith in her abilities! As soon as she'd returned to the rancho, Tía Dolores had had her piano moved into the family sala. The piano had come all the way from Mexico City, and

Josefina was eager to learn how to play it. So Tía
Dolores gave Josefina lessons. Right away, Josefina
had learned that making music on the piano was
much harder than it looked. But Tía Dolores was
generous with her encouragement. She never gave
up, no matter how Josefina fumbled at the keys.

Now Francisca frowned and rustled her
material. She made a great show of holding it up
to the fire and squinting as she stitched.

Clara glanced at the hem Francisca was
sewing. "Just look at the size of your stitches!"
she said. "They're much too big."

Francisca shrugged. "They'll hold the dress
together," she said.

"That's not the point," said Clara. "They *look*
bad."

"Oh, Clara!" said Francisca crossly. "The
stitches are on the inside! No one will see them."

"Yes, they will!" said Josefina, who didn't
like to hear her sisters squabble. "No one's dress
swirls more than yours at a dance, Francisca. And
no one is more admired!" Josefina whirled around
the room, pretending to be Francisca dancing. "See
my hem stitches?" she asked. She sang a dancing

song that had been one of Mamá's favorites.

Tía Dolores knew the song, too. She went straight to the piano and began to play it. Ana and Clara sang along and clapped in time to the music. Francisca tried not to smile. But when Josefina danced over to her, holding out both hands, Francisca happily thrust her sewing aside and sprang to her feet. Josefina and Francisca danced around the room, weaving in and out of the light of the fire. Soon Ana and Clara were dancing with each other, too. Tía Dolores played away merrily. Her *rebozo* slipped down from her shoulders. Her dark, shiny hair had a reddish luster in the firelight.

Tía Dolores was playing so loudly and they were all singing and laughing so much that none of them heard the door open. But it must have, because the next thing Josefina knew, Papá was there, tapping his foot in time to Tía Dolores's music. He watched the girls dance until the song was over. When they stopped, he folded his arms across his chest and pretended to scold. "Dancing instead of sewing?" he asked. He tried to look stern, but his eyes were full of fun. "Who started that *fandango*?"

rebozo

8

"I did, Papá!" said Josefina, flushed and breathless. "I was celebrating. I've finished my dress!"

"Good!" said Papá. "And a fine dress it is, too!"

"Gracias, Papá," said Josefina. She smoothed her dress with both hands. "The material comes from very far away. Tía Dolores gave it to us."

"How thoughtful of her!" said Papá. He turned to Tía Dolores. "You are very kind to my daughters. Gracias."

Tía Dolores looked pleased. "My father bought the material this summer from traders who came to

9

Santa Fe from the United States. The traders brought all sorts of things to trade—tools and clothes, paper and ink—"

"And pretty material!" Josefina added happily.

"*Sí*," said Papá. "I know about the *americanos* and the trail they follow. They first came to Santa Fe three years ago. Before that, it was illegal for them to come to New Mexico." He looked thoughtful. "I hope that trading with the americanos will be a good thing. I've heard that the traders need pack mules, so I'm raising some to take to Santa Fe next summer. I'll sell or swap the mules to get tools and other things we need on the rancho. It should be a profitable business."

"Oh, Papá," Josefina asked, "may we go to Santa Fe with you next summer?"

"Perhaps," said Papá, smiling at her eagerness. "But right now, I think all of you girls had better go to bed. I'm going to the village."

"In this storm?" asked Ana.

"It's because of the storm that I'm going," said Papá as he put on his hat. "I want to be sure Magdalena is all right." Tía Magdalena was Papá's sister. She was much older than he was, and she lived alone in the village about a mile from the rancho. "Her roof is not as strong as it should be, and her house is near the stream. I'm worried about flooding. Most of the time, nothing is more welcome than rain. But it's unusual for it to rain so late in the year, and such a hard rain can mean trouble."

Josefina listened. They'd been making so much noise, they hadn't noticed that the wind had an angry sound to it now, and the rain was coming down harder and harder. She watched Papá as he put on his woolen *sarape*. Even that wouldn't keep him dry tonight. Josefina turned a worried face up to Papá.

"Now, now. There's no need for you to worry, my Josefina," Papá said in his deep, comforting voice. "Our house is high above the stream. God will keep you safe, and your Tía Dolores is here to look after you."

sarape

"Sí, Papá," said Josefina. "But if the stream floods—"

"Our harvest is safely in," said Papá. "We'll move the animals to higher ground if we need to. Now come and say good night to me before I go."

The girls knelt before Papá, the palms and

11

fingers of their hands pressed together as for prayer.
Papá gave each girl his blessing and kissed her
praying hands. His smile was loving as he looked
down on his daughters' upturned faces. "Go to bed,"
he said. "The sky will be blue tomorrow."

Tía Dolores opened the door for Papá. "God
go with you," she said softly.

Papá nodded. Then he went out into the
windy, rainy night.

Papá had told Josefina not to worry, but she
could not obey. The sheepskins that were her bed
were warm and soft and comforting, but they could
not soothe away the worry that kept her awake. She
lay on her stomach with her chin on her clenched
hands and listened. Moment by moment the wind
grew wilder. It shrieked and howled and hurled the
rain against the roof and the walls as if it were trying
to destroy the house with its anger. Josefina shivered
at the sound of the storm's rage. *Please let Papá be
safe,* she prayed. *Please.* She was glad she couldn't
sleep. She hoped her prayers would protect Papá.

And so, when the church bell rang in the

night, Josefina was already awake. The bell's fast
clang, clang, clang came through the storm's uneven
gusts. It was faint but steady. Josefina
knew the church bell was an alarm. Its
clangs meant *danger, danger, danger!*

"Francisca! Clara!" said Josefina
urgently. "Wake up!" She stood and
began to put on her clothes.

Francisca groaned and pulled her blankets
over her head, but Clara sat up straight. "What's
the matter?" she asked Josefina.

"The church bell is ringing," said Josefina.
"Hurry! Get dressed. Papá may need our help."

The sisters dressed as fast as they could. Just
as they were finishing, Tía Dolores came to fetch
them. She was carrying a small candle. Her voice was
calm and very serious. She spoke against the sounds
of the storm with the same steady determination as
the ringing church bell. "Your papá is still down in
the village. I fear the church bell means the flooding
is bad there. I've wakened all the workers in the
house. Some will herd the animals to higher ground.
Others will try to build up the stream's banks so
that the stream won't flood the fields. I've told Ana

she must stay with her boys. But I want you girls to come with me. We must save as much as we can from the kitchen garden."

Josefina, Clara, and Francisca followed Tía Dolores. They were still under the cover of the roof when suddenly the sky was slashed in two by a jagged dagger of lightning. Its brilliant flash of light made everything white for a second. Then the light disappeared and the night seemed even darker than before. BOOM! A huge clap of thunder crashed so loudly it shook the house. Josefina stepped back, trembling.

"What's the matter?" Tía Dolores asked.

"It's the lightning," Francisca answered. "Josefina's afraid of it."

CRACK! Lightning split the sky again. Josefina couldn't move. All her life she had feared lightning. Mamá had understood. She would hug Josefina to her and wrap her rebozo around both of them. She'd cover Josefina's eyes with her hand so that Josefina wouldn't have to see the wicked flash of light or the plunge into darkness that followed. She'd hold Josefina so close that the beating of her heart almost blocked out the sound of the thunder.

CRACK! Lightning split the sky again. Josefina couldn't move.

Mamá! thought Josefina now, bracing herself for another flash. *Help me!*

Just then, Josefina felt Tía Dolores put a strong arm around her shoulders. Tía Dolores's little candle sputtered wildly in the wind, but it didn't go out. By its feeble light, Josefina saw Tía Dolores's gentle face. "Come with me, Josefina," she said.

Josefina took a shaky breath. She leaned close to Tía Dolores. Together, they stepped forward. Clara and Francisca followed behind. The rain put the little candle out. But Tía Dolores's step was sure, even in the darkness. She led the girls across the front courtyard, through the passageway, and into the back courtyard. As they passed Mamá's flowers, Josefina remembered what Tía Dolores had said when they'd worked together: *I know you can do it. I have faith in you.* Lightning sliced the sky and thunder boomed, again and again. Josefina shuddered, but Tía Dolores's arm gave her courage. She stayed within its safe hold as they went out the back gate to the kitchen garden.

Carmen, the cook, and her husband, Miguel, were already there filling big baskets with squash, beans, chiles, and pumpkins. The kitchen garden

 was awash in mud. It made Josefina sad to see it. She and her sisters had worked so hard all spring and summer tending the garden! She was sorry to pick the squash that were not perfectly ripe yet, but she knew it was better than letting them be washed away or rot from lying in water.

And there was so *much* water! A river of it rushed through the center of the garden, and the rain was still falling in torrents. Mud pulled at Josefina's moccasins and splashed up onto her legs. Soon she was soaked to the skin. Her hands were numb with cold and caked with dirt. Her arms were tired from lifting mud-streaked pumpkins, and her back hurt from carrying her heavy basket. Lightning flashed all around her and thunder rumbled. But Josefina bent to her work, trying to ignore the force and fury of the storm.

Tía Dolores has faith in me, Josefina said to herself. *I can't let her down.*

17

—

TURNING BLANKETS
INTO SHEEP

 Just as Papá promised, the sky was a
clean, clear blue the next morning.
Only a few gray clouds remained, and
they scuttled across the horizon as if they were
ashamed, shoving against each other in their hurry
to get away. Below, the ground was so wet it was
shiny, reflecting the new blue sky. It was crisscrossed
everywhere with thin little rivers no bigger than
trickles, trying to find their way down the hill back
to the stream.

Papá had come home from the village at dawn,
just in time for morning prayers. As she'd knelt in
front of the altar in the family sala, Josefina had
thanked God for Papá's safe return.

Now the family was gathered in the kitchen for breakfast. Josefina was helping Clara and Carmen, the cook, make *tortillas*. Ana was rocking her younger boy in a cradle that swung gently from the ceiling. Francisca was grinding corn. She would put a handful of dried corn on the flat *metate* stone and rub back and forth with the smaller *mano* stone until the corn was ground into coarse flour. As the cradle swung back and forth, it made a comforting *creak, creak, creak* sound, which the soft, regular *thud, thud, thud* of the mano matched in rhythm.

mano and metate

Papá looked tired. Tía Dolores gave him some mint tea. He sat down and took a long, grateful sip before he spoke.

"You all did a fine job of saving as much as you could from the garden," he said. "I'm afraid the news from the village is not as good. I was in time to save Magdalena's roof, but one whole corner of the church collapsed. Some of the villagers had not harvested yet, so their crops are lost. They were swept away by the stream when it rose over its banks."

"What a blessing it is that you brought our

19

harvest in early!" said Ana. "We'll be able to share it with the villagers who lost their crops. No one will go hungry this winter."

"Sí," said Papá. "That is a blessing." He paused as if he didn't want to say what he had to say next. At last he said sadly, "But we've suffered another loss. I was told about it late last night. It seems that the shepherds were moving our sheep from their summer grazing lands in the mountains down to the winter pastures closer to the rancho. When the storm began, the shepherds took a shortcut to save time. Just as they were crossing the bottom of a deep *arroyo*, a flash flood came. All of a sudden, the arroyo was full of a raging torrent of water. The water came so hard and so fast that the sheep couldn't get out of its way. The shepherds risked their lives to save as many sheep as they could. But hundreds of our sheep were drowned." As if he needed to hear it again to believe it, Papá repeated, "Hundreds of our sheep were drowned."

arroyo

Ana lifted her son out of the cradle and held him close. Everyone else was still. They looked at Papá, their faces full of concern. Then Josefina went

20

to stand by Papá's side. She put her hand on his arm and he patted it while he stared into the fire. So many sheep killed! Josefina knew that this was a terrible disaster. How cruel the storm had been! The rancho could not survive without sheep. They provided meat, and wool for weaving and for trading. What would Papá do?

Papá's voice was heavy with discouragement. "The sheep were very valuable," he said. "My father and grandfather built up the flocks over many years. It will take a long, long time for us to recover from this loss." He sighed. "We'll just have to start over.

21

I'll have to trade the mules I was raising. I have nothing else to trade. I'll have to use the mules to get new sheep so that we can increase our flocks again."

"Perhaps not," said Tía Dolores. She'd been so quiet, they'd almost forgotten she was there. Now she spoke to Papá, respectfully but firmly. "Forgive me for speaking, but perhaps it won't be necessary to trade the mules. Perhaps you could use the old sheep to get new sheep."

They all stared at her. "Please go on," said Papá.

Tía Dolores explained. "The old sheep provided you with sacks and sacks of wool when they were sheared last spring," she said. "Your storerooms are full of their fleece. What if we used that wool to weave as many blankets as we can? We'll keep as few as possible for our own use, and trade most of the blankets to the villagers for new sheep. We can trade with the Indians at the *pueblo, too.*

"But they all weave their own blankets," said Papá. "Why would they want more?"

pueblo "To trade to the americanos," answered Tía Dolores. "My father told me that they are glad to trade their goods for blankets. They value the blankets for their warmth and strength and beauty."

"I don't understand," said Francisca. "Who will do all of this weaving you talk about?"

Tía Dolores smiled. "We will," she said. "You and your sisters and I. The household servants will weave, and any workers on the rancho who are able."

Josefina saw that Francisca wasn't pleased with this answer, and Clara and Ana looked unsure. But Papá seemed to be giving the idea grave consideration. "Trading blankets for sheep," he said thoughtfully. "Perhaps it would be good for both sides. Our neighbors would help us by giving us the sheep we need. And *we* would help *them* by weaving blankets they can trade for goods that they need."

"Sí," said Tía Dolores simply.

Ana nudged Josefina with her elbow and raised her eyebrows. None of the sisters had ever heard Papá discuss business with a woman before. He was the *patrón*, the head of the rancho and the head of their family. He had never discussed business with Mamá. But Papá didn't seem to be offended by Tía Dolores's forwardness. Still, Josefina was not sure it was proper for Tía Dolores to have such a conversation with him. Josefina knew she and her sisters should sit quietly. They all knew it wasn't their place to speak.

All except Francisca, of course. "But Tía Dolores!" Francisca protested. "I don't see how we can weave any more than we already do! We hardly have time to do all our household chores as it is."

"We'll get up earlier," said Tía Dolores briskly. "If all four of you help—"

"Josefina can't help," said Francisca. "She doesn't know how to weave."

Ana nodded, and even Clara agreed with Francisca for once. "That's true," Clara said. "Mamá never taught her, because Josefina was too small. She's *still* too small to work the big loom."

"My servant, Teresita, weaves on a smaller loom that hangs from the ceiling," said Tía Dolores. "I'm sure she'd be willing to teach Josefina to weave on one like it. And I'm sure Josefina is big enough to do it. Josefina can help."

Josefina saw Papá looking at her. His smile said that he loved her even if he wasn't sure she could be of help with the weaving. With all her heart, Josefina wanted to please Papá. She could tell that Tía Dolores's idea had caught his interest and given him a little hope. She didn't want her sisters' doubts to discourage Papá—or Tía Dolores. And so she spoke up with spirit.

"I'd like to learn to use the small loom," she said. "And anyway, I can help wash and card and spin wool for the big loom. I know where to find the plants we use to make dye to color the wool, and . . . and Mamá always used to say that I was good at untangling knots."

Papá laughed out loud. His laugh was a sudden, unexpected, wonderful sound. "Well," he said to Tía Dolores. "If all of your weavers are as eager as my little Josefina, you'll turn the wool into blankets and the blankets into sheep in no time! I think we should give your plan a try."

Tía Dolores was very pleased. "We will pray for God's help," she said, "as we put His gifts to good use. Won't we, girls?"

Her smile was so happy, so full of energy and encouragement, that all the sisters had to smile back and say "Sí!" Even Francisca!

That very afternoon, Tía Dolores brought Josefina to Teresita. "Will you teach Josefina to weave?" she asked.

Teresita was working at a loom that hung near one wall and stretched from ceiling to floor. She looked at Josefina, and then she smiled. Teresita's smile seemed to use her whole face, because her eyes were surrounded by wrinkles of good humor. "Sí," she said.

"Gracias," said Tía Dolores. "You might as well begin right now. As I always say, 'The saints cry over lost time.'"

She left, and Teresita watched her go with a twinkle in her eye. Josefina could tell that she and Teresita were thinking the same thing—that Tía Dolores gave the saints very little reason to cry! She never wasted time!

Josefina sat down next to Teresita and watched her weave. After a little while Josefina asked, "How did you learn to weave?"

Teresita's voice was unhurried as she answered. "Before I came here with your Tía Dolores, I was a servant in your Abuelito's house in Santa Fe," she said. "But when I was a little girl, I lived with my people, the Navajos. My mamá taught me to weave on a loom like this. I've never forgotten, even though I was captured by enemies of the Navajos when I was about your age and taken from my family."

Josefina knew that the Navajo Indians lived in the mountains and deserts far to the west. "Did you ever see your mamá again?" she asked Teresita.

"No," said Teresita.

"Did you miss her?" asked Josefina.

"Sí," said Teresita. Her dark eyes met Josefina's. "You and I are alike in that way, aren't we?" she said. "We both lost our mamás at a young age."

Josefina nodded.

"I am sure you remember the things your mamá taught you," said Teresita.

Josefina nodded again. "Oh, sí!" she said. "My sisters and I try very hard to remember her lessons and stories and songs."

"Good," said Teresita. She was quiet for a long moment. With a light touch, she ran her hand across the loom. Then she said, "Here is a story my mamá told me. When the world was new, Spider Woman taught the Navajos to weave on a loom like this one. The upper crosspiece is the sky bar. The lower crosspiece is the earth bar, and this stick, which goes between the strands of yarn, is a sunbeam. I'll show you how it works."

Josefina watched. The loom looked like a tall harp. Long, taut strands of wool yarn connected the sky bar to the earth bar. The sunbeam stick held the strands apart. It made space between the strands so that Teresita could weave another piece of wool through them. When she had woven the wool through all the long strands, Teresita pulled the wool gently, pushed it down into place, then turned it and wove it back in the other direction. Teresita's hands made it look easy. Josefina could not wait to try. "May I do it?" she asked.

Teresita handed her the wool. "Remember," she said, "the earth, the sky, and the sun have already worked hard to provide us with this wool by growing grass for the sheep to eat. They didn't hurry their work, and neither should you."

Josefina worked very slowly indeed, but even so, the row she wove was loose and bumpy. Teresita helped her take it out and do it over again.

Josefina was weaving a straight row that was a pale gray color. But the part of the blanket that

Teresita's hands made weaving look easy.
Josefina could not wait to try.

Teresita had woven had a lovely pattern of stripes and zigzagging lines and diamond shapes and triangles on it. The dark blue zigzags reminded Josefina of the mountains that surrounded the rancho, and the creamy white zigzags just above them looked like the snow that capped the mountains. Floating below the zigzag mountains were dark V's that looked just like the graceful wild geese Josefina saw flying across the autumn sky. And below them, Teresita had woven pale golden shapes that reminded Josefina of the cottonwood leaves that fell all around her when she went to the stream every morning. Most of the colors of the blanket were soft—deep browns, many gentle shades of gray and blue, and delicate gold and yellow. But every few rows, Teresita had woven in a yarn that was the fiery orange-red of the harvest moon. "The pattern is so pretty," said Josefina. "It reminds me of our rancho."

"Yes," said Teresita, wrinkling up her eyes in a smile. "A blanket should be as beautiful as the place it comes from." She was thoughtful for a while before she said, "Maybe this blanket will travel all the way to the United States. Maybe some little girl there will look at it, and then she will know how beautiful it is here in New Mexico."

Josefina liked that idea. "She'll probably like the red strands the best," she said, "just as I do. They stand out from all the rest."

"They do," said Teresita. "But every strand, dull or bright, is part of the pattern. Every strand adds to the strength and beauty of the whole blanket."

"Sí," agreed Josefina. "But the red wool seems to change everything around it somehow. It makes all the colors look better."

That first day, Josefina had to do her row of weaving over and over again before it was smooth and even. But Teresita was very patient, and slowly, slowly, Josefina's hands became accustomed to the feeling of the wool. When Josefina came for her next weaving lesson, Teresita had set up a loom for her to use by herself.

Josefina enjoyed her weaving lessons with Teresita. It was a pleasure to weave the wool through the strands, and to push the newly woven row down so that it fit snugly next to the row below it. Part of the pleasure was knowing that with each row, Josefina was adding to a blanket that would help

Papá replace the sheep he'd lost. Josefina was pleased and proud to be of help to her family. And as the days went by and she learned to be a better weaver, she was pleased and proud of herself for learning something new. *I may be the youngest and the smallest, but I can help, just like my sisters,* she thought. *I can help turn blankets into sheep! Tía Dolores was right.*

Sometimes as she was weaving, Josefina smiled to herself, thinking of Tía Dolores. It seemed to Josefina that Tía Dolores was like the beautiful bright red wool. She changed everything around her and made it better.

RABBIT BRUSH

Follow me!" Josefina shouted happily. She ran up the hill as swift and light as a bird skimming over a stream. The air at the top smelled of juniper and *piñón.* It was pure and cool and thin and sweet. Josefina turned around and called back to her sisters, "Wait till you see! There's *lots* of rabbit brush up here!"

Josefina and her sisters were on an expedition to gather wildflowers, herbs, roots, barks, berries, and leaves. They'd use them to make dyes to color the wool for weaving. Teresita had told Josefina that the Navajos used rabbit brush blossoms to make many shades of yellow. Ana, Francisca, and Clara were not far behind Josefina on the path. Josefina was glad it was almost time for the mid-day meal. She knew that Carmen, the cook, had packed tortillas, onions, squash, goat cheese, and plums for them to eat. The canteen was full of cold water to drink. Miguel, Carmen's husband, was carrying the food and the canteen. He had come along to be sure the girls were safe.

"Oh!" said Ana when she reached the top of the hill. "Isn't it pretty up here!" Josefina thought Ana looked very pretty herself! She was a little breathless, and her cheeks were reddened by the climb and the wind.

All the sisters seemed to be in high spirits. They set to work gathering rabbit brush, delighted to be out in the bracing air and bright sunshine. Clara, who usually liked to keep her feet firmly on the ground, seemed to have a bounce in her step today. And Francisca, who was usually so careful of her appearance, didn't seem to care that her hair was windblown and tousled and had a yellow leaf caught in it.

rabbit brush

"Look," said Josefina. She took the leaf out of Francisca's hair and twirled it on its stem. The leaf was such a sunny yellow, Josefina thought about saving it to put in her memory box along with the pretty swallow's feather she'd found earlier. She kept things that reminded her of Mamá in her memory box. Mamá had loved swallows, and she had loved autumn, too, when the bright yellow leaves stood out against the dark green of the mountainsides and shimmered against the deep blue sky. But Josefina knew that the little leaf would soon turn brown and crumble, so she let it go. She watched the breeze catch it and send it swooping and flying as if it were a tiny yellow bird.

swallow's feather

Josefina loved autumn as much as Mamá had. It was a busy time on the rancho. All the harvested crops had to be stored properly to preserve them for the winter. The storeroom was full of garlic, onions, beans, corn, squash, pumpkins, cheeses, and meats. The adobe bins in the *granero* were full of grain to be ground into flour. Josefina and her sisters had made strings of squash slices, apple slices, red chiles, and herbs. The strings would hang near the hearth where they would dry and be handy for use in cooking throughout the winter. Josefina always enjoyed the cheerful bustle in the kitchen at harvest time, but it was a treat to be out and away today, high up on this golden hillside with her sisters.

The morning had flown by. Now it was mid-day and the sisters gathered around the food Carmen had packed for them. Miguel found a sunny spot nearby and took his afternoon rest while the girls ate.

Josefina bit into a plum that was warm from the sunshine. The breeze lifted her hair off her back and cooled her face. "I wish Tía Dolores had been able to come with us today," she said. "She'd enjoy this." Tía Dolores had gone to the village. She was bringing food to some of the villagers who had lost their crops in the flood.

"Sí!" agreed Ana and Clara. Francisca had a mouthful of tortilla.

Josefina grinned. She took a sprig of rabbit brush out of her basket and pretended to be Tía Dolores. "We'll put these flowers to good use, won't we, girls?" she said, imitating Tía Dolores's energetic manner. Ana and Clara laughed, especially when Josefina put the flowers to good use tickling them!

But Francisca grabbed the flowers away.

"Whenever Tía Dolores talks about putting things to good use, it always ends up meaning more work for us," she grumbled. "All this weaving, for example."

Josefina smiled. "I *like* the weaving," she said.

"Well," said Francisca. "It's new to you. But I find it very dull." She collapsed back on the grass and fanned herself with the sprig of flowers. "I'm worn out from it!"

"Now, Francisca," Ana scolded in her kindly, motherly way. "You have plenty of energy for things you enjoy, like dancing. Pretend you're dancing while you work at the loom. Dance on the treadles!"

"I can't dance very well with the loom!" said Francisca shortly.

"You don't weave very well with the loom, either," said Clara. "Weaving is just the sort of slow, patient work you're not good at, Francisca."

Francisca made a face. "Work!" she said. "I thought that when Tía Dolores came, there would be *less* work for us, not *more*."

"She doesn't ask us to do any more than she does herself," said Clara.

"You're right," said Francisca, sitting up. "Tía Dolores is always at work. She's always trying to fix

Francisca grabbed the flowers. "Whenever Tía Dolores talks about putting things to good use, it always means more work for us," she grumbled.

things and improve things and change things—especially *us!*" Francisca poked and prodded Clara's arm with the sprig of rabbit brush as she continued to complain. "Tía Dolores is always trying to poke and prod us into being different than we are. She's never satisfied. She always thinks we can be better."

"Tía Dolores came to teach us," said Ana. "She's not a servant."

"She certainly is not," agreed Francisca. "She seems to think she is the *patrona!* Look at how she's put herself in charge of the weaving business." Tía Dolores had also taken on the responsibility of keeping track of the number of blankets the rancho was producing.

"As Papá said, we must replace the sheep," Ana said calmly. She collected the remains of the food, and the girls started back down the hill with Miguel. Ana walked next to Francisca. "We should be grateful to Tía Dolores for her good idea and her hard work. She is helping us, and that is *exactly* what we asked her to do."

Francisca frowned. "Tía Dolores's help is not *exactly* what I expected it to be," she said. "Tía Dolores isn't, either. She seems different than she was when she came here the first time."

"Yes!" said Josefina. She turned around and walked backwards a few steps so that she could face her sisters. "Tía Dolores seems happier."

"I think she is," said Ana. "She even looks happier, and prettier, too. She's not so thin and pale as she was."

"She's letting her skin get rough and red," said Francisca, who was vain about her own complexion.

Josefina did not like to hear Francisca criticize Tía Dolores. "Why are you speaking this way about Tía Dolores?" she asked Francisca. "You were the one who used to say that she was elegant and that her clothes were beautiful."

"She never wears those beautiful clothes anymore," said Francisca, "just everyday work clothes." She shook her head and said mournfully, "Soon, I expect none of us will have anything *but* worn out, workaday clothes."

Clara snorted. "You'd have a fancy new dress if you'd ever settle down and finish it!" she said.

Francisca ignored her. "Tía Dolores is determined to weave all our wool into blankets," she said. "I'm sure she won't spare even enough for new sashes for us. Not that it matters how we look. We don't have time to do anything but work these days! We're up long before dawn—"

"Ah, that's it!" said Ana. "You are out of sorts because you have to get up so early!" Ana, Clara, and Josefina glanced at each other and hid their smiles. Francisca was well known for being slow to rise in the morning. Ana went on, "Mamá always said no one has a sweeter temper than you do, Francisca—as long as you have plenty of sleep!"

Josefina noticed that when Ana mentioned Mamá, a strange look crossed Francisca's face. Francisca started to say something, but then she seemed to change her mind. She said nothing.

Josefina took hold of Francisca's hand and swung it as they walked together. "Remember the morning song Mamá used to sing to you to help you wake up?" she asked Francisca.

Ever so briefly, the strange look crossed Francisca's face again. Then she began to sing, "Arise in the morning . . ." She stopped. "How did it go?" she asked. "I've forgotten. Sing it for me, Josefina."

Josefina began to sing:

Here comes the dawn,
now it gives us the light of day.
Arise in the morning
and see that day has dawned.

Josefina sang the song in her clear, sweet voice as the girls made their way down the hill. Tía Dolores met them as they passed the orchard. She was carrying a basket full of apples, walking with her usual purposeful stride. Wisps of her ruddy auburn hair curled out from under her rebozo, and her skirt flapped in the wind.

"Josefina," she said. "I do love to hear you sing!" She smiled. "Perhaps you'll sing a special song for all the village to hear as part of the Christmas celebration this year."

Josefina could feel her own smile sink right off her face. "Oh, no, Tía Dolores!" she said quickly, too surprised to be polite. She spoke again, this time with more respect. "I mean, I beg your pardon, but no, thank you."

"Why not?" asked Tía Dolores. "A lovely voice

like yours is a gift from God. I am sure God means you to use it to delight others, especially if you do so to celebrate Him."

Josefina thought of how it would feel to have everyone looking at her, everyone listening to her singing all alone. She shivered. It was scarier than lightning. "I'm . . . sorry," she said, stumbling over the words. "I just *couldn't*."

Tía Dolores looked Josefina straight in the eye. "You mean you don't *want* to," she said. "But perhaps one day you will."

Josefina felt something jab her arm. It was the sprig of rabbit brush, and Francisca was poking her with it. Francisca raised one eyebrow and gave Josefina a look that said, *You see? Remember what I said about Tía Dolores poking and prodding us to be different than we are? Wasn't I right?*

THE FIRST LOVE

malacate

A few nights later, Josefina sat on a stool close to the fire in the family sala. The evening air had a sharpness that warned of the wintry cold to come. Josefina curled up her toes inside her warm knitted socks. She and Clara were spinning wool into yarn. They were using long spindles called *malacates* to twist tufts of wool into one long strand of yarn as the wool spun around. Ana was putting her boys to bed. Francisca sat nearby sewing her fancy dress, which, as Clara had pointed out, she *still* had not finished.

Tía Dolores was at her writing desk, bent close to her work. *Scritch, scratch, scritch, scratch.* Josefina loved the sound Tía Dolores's quill pen made as she wrote in the ledger she used to keep track of the weaving business. Paper and ink were precious, so Tía Dolores made her numbers small and filled every inch of every page. Papá sat nearby at the table, quietly watching her write.

Josefina looked around the family sala. *A piano, a writing desk, paper, pen, ink, and a ledger!* she thought. *Tía Dolores has brought so many new things to this room, Mamá wouldn't recognize it!* But Tía Dolores's things were not the only changes. Papá looked different, too. His face looked less tired, as if he were not so weighed down with sorrow as he had been.

"There!" said Tía Dolores. She put her pen down with a pleased expression. "Would you do me the honor of looking at the figures?" she asked Papá.

"Sí," said Papá. Tía Dolores brought the ledger to the table, and she and Papá looked at it together.

"This shows how many sacks of wool we have," explained Tía Dolores as she pointed to a column of figures in the ledger. "And this shows how many blankets I think we can weave. And this shows how many sheep we'll get when we trade the blankets."

Papá nodded. "Excellent," he said. "The weaving business should do very well, God willing. I am grateful to you, Dolores."

"Your daughters have worked hard," she said.

"Sí," said Papá. "They weave. But you have taken care of all this." He patted the ledger. "It is fortunate that you can read and write."

"My aunt taught me when I lived with her in Mexico City," said Tía Dolores. She thought for a moment, and then she said, "And now, with your permission, I'll teach your daughters to read and write. Then they will be able to continue the weaving business after I have left."

Francisca gasped. Josefina knew that meant she was not happy at the thought of yet another new thing to do. Now they would have lessons in reading and writing on top of everything else!

Tía Dolores must have heard and understood the gasp, too, because she said, "The lessons won't add any time to the day. I have a little speller I brought with me from Mexico City. We'll use it when we sit by the fire at night. We will be putting our evenings to *very* good use."

Francisca spoke up boldly. "I don't see the

need for learning to read and write," she said. "I have no time to read books, and no one ever sends letters that have anything to do with *me*."

Tía Dolores smiled. "Ah, but soon they will, Francisca!" she said. "Soon your papá will be receiving letters from young men who want to marry you."

Francisca sniffed. "Hmph!" she said. "I won't read them! And I'll reply to any marriage proposal by handing the young man the squash."

"That's true," stated Clara. "She's already done it!" In fact, a young man had already proposed to Francisca. She had indeed followed the old custom of giving him a squash to let him know she was not interested in marrying him.

"Letters proposing marriage can be very persuasive," said Tía Dolores. "Your papá won your mamá's heart with his letters!"

Francisca's dark eyes were flinty. "Mamá could not read," she said.

"No," said Tía Dolores. "But she always said that she loved the way your papá signed his name with such fancy flourishes."

Papá laughed. "I was young and foolish," he

said. "It was the custom to make flourishes to show what an important person you were, and to make your signature different from anyone else's. I don't bother with flourishes anymore."

"Please won't you show us how you used to do it, Papá?" asked Josefina.

Papá smiled but shook his head. "No, no. It's a waste of paper," he said.

"Not at all," said Tía Dolores. She handed him the pen and the green glass inkwell.

"Very well," said Papá agreeably. Josefina stood next to him and Clara peered over his shoulder. As they watched, Papá wrote his name in handsome, upright letters. Then, under his name, Papá made graceful swirls and curving spirals that looked like a long, lovely curl of ribbon.

"Oh, Papá, it's beautiful!" said Josefina. She turned to Tía Dolores. "Will we really learn to write like that?" she asked.

"Sí!" said Tía Dolores. "We'll begin tomorrow."

Josefina stared at Papá's beautiful writing. Then she looked up to smile at Francisca. Surely Francisca would enjoy learning to do something as fancy and elegant-looking as this!

As they watched, Papá wrote his name in handsome, upright letters.
Then, under his name, Papá made graceful swirls and curving spirals.

But Francisca was gone. She had slipped out quietly, without saying good night or waiting for Papá's blessing.

Something woke Josefina in the middle of the night. It was a sound, just a small sound, but one that made Josefina sit up and tilt her head and listen hard. As her eyes adjusted to the darkness, Josefina saw that Francisca was not in her bed. Quietly, so as not to wake Clara, Josefina pulled on her moccasins and wrapped herself in her blanket. She crept outside. Francisca was sitting in the courtyard. She was wrapped in her blanket, too. There was no moon, but the stars were so big and bright Josefina could see Francisca's face. It was streaked with tears.

Josefina was surprised. She had not seen Francisca cry since Mamá died. "Francisca!" Josefina whispered as she came near. "What's the matter?"

"Go away," said Francisca fiercely.

Josefina knelt down next to her sister. "Are you hurt?" she asked. "Are you ill? Shall I fetch Tía Dolores?"

50

"No!" said Francisca. She spoke with such force Josefina was startled. Her voice sounded hard as she said, "I've had quite enough of Tía Dolores!"

"What do you mean?" asked Josefina.

Francisca wiped the tears off her cheeks with an impatient hand. "Don't you see what's happening?" she asked. "Has Tía Dolores's praise for your sewing and weaving made you blind? Has she made you feel like such an important person that you don't care how she's changing everything? Nothing is the same as it was when Mamá was alive." Suddenly the bitterness left Francisca's voice. It was replaced by sadness. "Every change makes Mamá seem farther and farther away," she said. "Every change makes me feel as if I'm losing Mamá again. And oh, Josefina! I miss Mamá so!"

"So do I," said Josefina passionately. Her heart ached with sympathy for Francisca. Now she saw why Francisca had complained about Tía Dolores. Josefina tried to make Francisca feel better. "I miss Mamá, too," she said. "But Tía Dolores is good and kind! She is only trying to help us."

"By changing us!" said Francisca. "Now she's going to make us learn to read and write. Mamá

51

didn't read or write. Mamá didn't ask anyone to teach *us* to read or write. Reading and writing will be one more way Tía Dolores will pull us away from Mamá. It'll be just one more way she'll fill our heads and our hearts so that we'll have no room left for Mamá. We'll start to forget her. We've already started."

"Oh, Francisca!" said Josefina. "That's not true!" But a dark fear stole into Josefina's mind. Was Francisca right? It was true that Tía Dolores had changed their lives. Josefina herself had changed. Hadn't she braved the lightning? Hadn't she learned to weave? But did Tía Dolores's new ideas and new ways mean there was no room for the old ways? *Was* Tía Dolores making them forget Mamá?

Francisca straightened her shoulders. "I am not going to do it," she said firmly. "I won't learn to read and write." She stood up and looked down at Josefina. "You'll have to make your own choice," she said. "Decide for yourself." Then she left.

Josefina stayed alone in the courtyard. She looked up at the huge, endless black sky and felt as if she were adrift in it. The stars seemed to be all around her—above her and below her and surrounding her on every side. Josefina felt lost. Francisca made it sound as if learning to read would be disloyal to Mamá. She made it seem as if Josefina had to choose between Mamá and Tía Dolores, between the old and the new.

What should I do, Mamá? Josefina asked. But she knew there would be no answer. The stars were as silent as stones.

Usually Josefina skipped and sang all the way to the stream on laundry day. But today she walked joylessly, thinking about the conversation she'd had with Francisca the night before.

Tía Dolores was waiting for Josefina by the stream. "There you are, Josefina!" she said cheerfully. "You're as quiet as a little shadow this morning. And where are your sisters?"

"They're helping Carmen in the kitchen," Josefina answered.

"Good!" said Tía Dolores. "Then after we do the laundry, you will have your first reading lesson by yourself!"

Josefina tried to smile.

If Tía Dolores noticed that Josefina was not paying much attention to the clothes she was washing, she was too kind to say anything about it. They worked in an unusual silence. Tía Dolores spread a freshly-washed white cloth on a bush to dry. There were already three other white cloths on the bush. "Look, Josefina!" said Tía Dolores with laughter in her voice. "They're four white doves perched on a rosemary bush!"

Josefina's face lit up for the first time that day. "Oh!" she said. "Mamá used to say that poem sometimes!" She tried to recite the whole poem.

"Behold four little white doves, perched on a rosemary bush, they were . . . they were . . . " Josefina faltered. "I can't remember the rest," she said sadly.

Tía Dolores nodded. "Don't let it trouble you," she said. She draped another cloth on the bush.

Josefina sighed so deeply and so unhappily that Tía Dolores gave her a questioning look. "Oh, Tía Dolores," Josefina said, full of misery. "It *does* worry me. I can keep things that remind me of Mamá in my memory box, but I can't keep her words anywhere, and I'm beginning to forget them. It makes me afraid that I'm beginning to forget Mamá herself."

Tía Dolores's eyes were gentle as she listened. When Josefina stopped talking, Tía Dolores dried her hands on her skirt and said, "Come with me, Josefina."

Josefina almost had to run to keep up with Tía Dolores's long strides. Tía Dolores led Josefina back to the house and into the family sala. Her writing desk was still there on its stand. Without saying a word, Tía Dolores opened the lid of the writing desk and pulled out a drawer. From a secret compartment in the drawer she took a little book bound in soft brown leather. She handed it to Josefina.

Very, very carefully, Josefina turned the pages of the book. She couldn't read the words, but on many pages there were little sketches. Josefina stopped when she came to a drawing of four white birds perched on a bush.

Tía Dolores read the words on the page aloud:

> *Behold four little white doves*
> *perched on a rosemary bush.*
> *They were saying to each other,*
> *"There's no love like the first love."*

As she listened, Josefina remembered hearing Mamá's own dear voice, low and lilting and full of love, saying those very words.

"Your mamá didn't read or write," said Tía Dolores. "She learned this poem by hearing our papá read it aloud to us when we were little girls. When I was in Mexico City, I made this book. In it I wrote prayers, poems, songs, stories, even funny sayings your mamá and I both loved when we were girls. It helped me feel close to her, even though I was far away." She smiled at Josefina. "When you learn to read and write, you can look in this book any time you like and read your mamá's words. In it you can write things you remember her saying. This book will be a place to keep her words safe, so that you'll never lose them."

Josefina smiled with tremendous relief and gladness. She felt as if she had received an answer from Mamá herself about what she should do. It was as if Mamá were encouraging her to learn to read and write. Francisca was wrong. Reading and writing wouldn't pull them away from Mamá, it would help them remember her. "Oh, please will you teach me to read this book?" Josefina asked Tía Dolores.

"This book and any other you like!" said Tía Dolores. "Reading is a way to hold on to the past, to travel to places you've never been, and to learn about worlds beyond your own time or experience. You'll find there are many grander books than this one! Would you like to keep this little book with your memory box to be your very own?"

"No, gracias," said Josefina. She smiled a little smile. "That wouldn't be putting it to good use!

"When you learn to read and write," said Tía Dolores, "you can look in this book any time you like and read your mamá's words. It will be a place to keep her words safe, so that you'll never lose them."

I think you ought to keep it and read to all of us from it sometimes."

"Very well," said Tía Dolores.

"But may I borrow it for a moment?" Josefina asked. "I'll be careful."

"Sí, of course!" said Tía Dolores.

"Gracias!" said Josefina.

With a light heart and light feet, Josefina ran to find Francisca. She was sweeping in the kitchen.

"Look, Francisca!" said Josefina breathlessly. She opened Tía Dolores's little book to the drawing of the four doves. "The words on this page are Mamá's poem about the four doves," she said. "Do you remember it?"

Francisca thought. "Just the last line," she said. "I think it ends, 'There's no love like the first love.'"

"Sí!" said Josefina. "This whole book is filled with prayers and poems and sayings of Mamá's. Tía Dolores made it. Don't you see, Francisca? When we can read this book, it will be like hearing Mamá's voice. And when we can write, we can add things we remember her saying. This book will be a place to keep her words safe forever." Josefina put the book into Francisca's hands.

Francisca looked at the book and smiled. She didn't say anything, but her eyes were shining.

Josefina smiled back. "Come with me," she said. "Perhaps Tía Dolores will read more to us."

The two sisters hurried to the family sala. "Tía Dolores," said Josefina. "Francisca would like to hear you read something of Mamá's from your book. Would you read to us?"

"With pleasure," answered Tía Dolores. "But first, I would like to write your names in the book."

Francisca and Josefina watched eagerly while Tía Dolores dipped her pen in the ink. "This is your name, Francisca," she said.

Scritch, scratch, the pen moved across the page in the small book. "And now I'll write your name, Josefina."

"Be sure to add lots of flourishes," said Francisca, "to show what an important person she is!"

"I will!" said Tía Dolores. She wrote:

María Josefina Montoya

Looking
Back
1824

A PEEK INTO
THE PAST

When Josefina was a girl, only a few New Mexican villages had schools. Some well-to-do families could afford to hire a private tutor for their children or send them to schools and universities in Mexico City. In some Pueblo Indian villages, Catholic priests ran mission schools for Indian children. But most New Mexicans who could read and write probably learned just the way Josefina did—from a family member who taught them at home.

This writing desk is plain on the outside—but inside, it is beautifully painted and carved and filled with small drawers.

Children in Josefina's time would have mastered reading before they learned to write. Children began learning to read by using spellers and simple readers

called *silabarios*, which showed examples and pictures of common words. As their reading skill improved,

*This illustration from a **silabario** shows words beginning with each letter of the alphabet. The Spanish alphabet is not the same as the English one. Can you find the letters that are different?*

children usually practiced reading from prayer books.

In Josefina's time, people wrote with a *quill pen* made from a long feather. They dipped the point of the quill into ink made from charcoal, soot, or powdered ink mixed with water. Some settlers kept their ink in a fancy *inkwell* made of silver or china, but many people used an *inkhorn*—a deer's antler that was hollowed out and plugged with a wooden stopper. A writing desk like Tía Dolores's would have been a prized possession.

Quill pen and inkwell

Paper and books were precious, too. Families who owned books treasured them, because they were so hard to get. They had to be carried hundreds of miles over the *Camino Real,* the rugged wagon trail from Mexico City to New Mexico. Even so, many settlers owned prayer books, and some

This prayer book belonged to a New Mexican family. It was printed in Mexico City in 1723.

63

One of the best-loved books in Josefina's time was the great Spanish novel Don Quixote. Here the main character, Don Quixote, sets off on an adventure with his faithful friend Sancho Panza beside him.

people had books of history, science, law, agriculture, poetry, and popular literature.

In New Mexico, writing was especially important for legal records, such as wills and court cases. When people signed their names, they often added their own special design or flourish—just as Papá did. The fancy flourish, called a *rubric*, made a person's signature easy to recognize but very hard for someone else to copy.

Can you read these signatures written by women in Josefina's time? They are María Martínez, Doña Leonor Domínguez, and Josefa Madrid.

Whether or not New Mexicans learned to read and write, they received many kinds of education as they grew up. From their mothers, aunts, and grandmothers, girls learned the skills they needed to run a home of their own. A nine-year-old girl like Josefina would already know a great deal about sewing,

Girls learned household skills at an early age. This girl is sewing while she sits in the courtyard of her home.

knitting, spinning, weaving, cooking, gardening, and preserving food for the winter. Most boys learned skills they would need for farming or ranching. They learned to water the fields, plant and harvest crops, tend animals, and repair buildings and farm tools. Some boys became

apprentices, or students of tradesmen, so they could learn to become weavers, blacksmiths, or tailors.

This boy is learning how to water the family's crops. His father is teaching him to open an irrigation ditch, or **acequia,** *to let water flow into a field. Crops could not grow without water from the acequias.*

65

New Mexicans also taught their children about faith in God and about the Catholic religion. Most families prayed together every morning and evening, and children began learning prayers at an early age. Children learned from priests, too. In Josefina's day, smaller villages usually received a visit from a priest only a few times a year, but in bigger towns like Santa Fe, priests were available year round and taught classes for children on religion and other subjects.

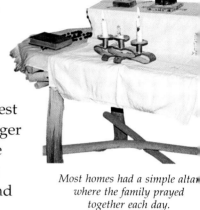

Most homes had a simple altar where the family prayed together each day.

This engraving from the 1870s shows a priest teaching a small group of children. In Josefina's time, classes much like this were held in larger towns like Santa Fe.

Children also learned lessons about good behavior through engaging stories called *cuentos* and sayings called *dichos*. Tía Dolores loved the dicho "The saints cry over lost time," and she said it often to remind her nieces to keep busy. Even if parents could not read and write, they knew hundreds of stories, sayings, poems, and songs by heart and taught them to their children.

Musicians and poets were almost always featured at village events like dances, weddings, and baptisms, and sometimes villagers performed traditional plays. Some songs, poems, and plays had religious themes, and others told of Spanish kings and queens and the history of Spain.

All of these traditions were important and entertaining ways for children to learn about their history and the values that were important to New Mexican settlers.

Many of the settlers' songs told about their history and faith. Musicians performed such songs at dances and celebrations.

GLOSSARY OF SPANISH WORDS

Abuelito *(ah-bweh-LEE-toh)*—Grandpa

acequia *(ah-SEH-kee-ah)*—a ditch made to carry water to a farmer's fields

adobe *(ah-DOH-beh)*—a building material made of earth mixed with straw and water. Most New Mexican houses were built of adobe.

americano *(ah-meh-ree-KAH-no)*—a man from the United States

arroyo *(ah-RO-yo)*—a gully or dry riverbed with steep sides

Camino Real *(kah-MEE-no rey-AHL)*—the main road or trail that ran from Mexico City to New Mexico. Its name means "Royal Road."

cuento *(KWEN-toh)*—a story or folktale

dicho *(DEE-cho)*—a proverb or wise saying

Don Quixote *(dohn kee-HO-teh)*—the title of a famous Spanish novel written in the early 1600s. It means "Sir Quixote."

fandango *(fahn-DAHN-go)*—a big celebration or party that includes a lively dance

gracias *(GRAH-see-ahs)*—thank you

granero *(grah-NEH-ro)*—a room used for storing grain, such as wheat and corn

malacate *(mah-lah-KAH-teh)*—a long, thin spindle used to spin wool into yarn. New Mexicans used malacates instead of spinning wheels.

mano *(MAH-no)*—a stone that is held in the hand and used to grind corn. Dried corn is put on a large flat stone called a *metate*, and then the mano is rubbed back and forth over the corn to break it down into flour.

metate *(meh-TAH-teh)*—a large flat stone used with a *mano* to grind corn

patrón *(pah-TROHN)*—a man who has earned respect because he owns land and manages it well, and is a good leader of his family and his workers

patrona *(pah-TROH-nah)*—a woman who has the responsibilities of a *patrón*

piñón *(pee-NYOHN)*—a kind of short, scrubby pine that produces delicious nuts

pueblo *(PWEH-blo)*—a village of Pueblo Indians

rancho *(RAHN-cho)*—a farm or ranch where crops are grown and animals are raised

rebozo *(reh-BO-so)*—a long shawl worn by girls and women

sala *(SAH-lah)*—a large room in a house

Santa Fe *(SAHN-tah FEH)*—the capital city of New Mexico. Its name means "Holy Faith."

sarape *(sah-RAH-peh)*—a warm blanket that is wrapped around the shoulders or worn as a poncho

sí *(SEE)*—yes

silabario *(see-lah-BAH-ree-o)*—a simple reading book that helps teach the sounds of the letters of the alphabet

tía *(TEE-ah)*—aunt

tortilla *(tor-TEE-yah)*—a kind of flat, round bread made of corn or wheat

F
TR

C.2

$11.95

Tripp, Valerie.

Josefina learns a
lesson.

32082000512848

DATE			
			4/99